OLIVIA

Best Sister Ever

Adapted by R. J. Cregg
Based on the screenplay written by Andy Guerdat and Steve Sullivan
Illustrated by Patrick Spaziante

Simon Spotlight
New York   London   Toronto   Sydney   New Delhi

Based on the TV series OLIVIA™ as seen on Nickelodeon™

SIMON SPOTLIGHT
An imprint of Simon & Schuster Children's Publishing Division
1230 Avenue of the Americas, New York, New York 10020
This Simon Spotlight paperback edition May 2017
OLIVIA™ Ian Falconer Ink Unlimited, Inc. and © 2017 Ian Falconer and Classic Media, LLC
All rights reserved, including the right of reproduction in whole or in part in any form.
SIMON SPOTLIGHT and colophon are registered trademarks of Simon & Schuster, Inc.
For information about special discounts for bulk purchases, please contact
Simon & Schuster Special Sales at 1-866-506-1949 or business@simonandschuster.com.
Manufactured in the United States of America 0417 LAK
1 2 3 4 5 6 7 8 9 10
ISBN 978-1-4814-8895-2
ISBN 978-1-4814-8896-9 (eBook)

"My plan for William's first birthday party is almost complete," Olivia told her mother. "Finish his card—check!" she said.

"I think that's your prettiest, most glittery one yet!" Mother said.

"Now I need to make a present to go with it," Olivia said.

"The party's not until this afternoon," Mother said. "I'm sure you'll think of something wonderful."

Wonderful? Olivia thought.
*It has to be perfect! First
birthdays are extra special.
But what does William want?*
Olivia wondered.

Olivia imagined hosting the Ultimate Baby Stuff Spectacular.
"Get ready to be amazed!" she said. "I bet you'll go goo-goo over my
new . . . Whatever-in-the-World-William-Could-Possibly-Want . . . in a Box!"
William and the crowd went wild, but Olivia couldn't give William an
imaginary invention.

William reached for his big sister. "I love you, too," Olivia said. "There's got to be a way to find out what you really want."

Then she had a stupendous idea. "It's time to become a birthday detective!" she said.

"Agent Double-Oh-Livia reporting," Olivia said into her recorder.
"Operation Perfect Present starts now."
"Operation what?" her brother Ian asked.
"Operation Perfect Present," Olivia repeated. "Our assignment is to find out what William really loves. Then I'll know exactly what he wants for his birthday."

"So far Birthday Baby likes sitting and crawling," Olivia said as she peered through her binoculars.
William picked up Perry's dog bone and banged it against his dish.

"And making noise!" Ian said.

"And making noise," Olivia agreed.

Olivia and Ian watched as their father fixed the kitchen sink.

"Got it!" Father said as he pulled his head out from under the counter.
William suddenly giggled. His father's head was covered in goop from the pipes!
"And he likes head goop," Olivia noted.

"Operation Perfect Present continues." Olivia whispered outside William's room a few minutes later. "What Birthday Baby wants is still unknown." She spied on him with a mirror.

"Birthday Baby doesn't want a nap," Ian added.

William clanked his rattle on his crib. In the mirror Olivia could see William reaching for her.

"He sees us!" she said. "Cover blown. Agent Double-Oh-Livia signing off."

"Hi, William," Olivia said. "I'm stumped," she said to Ian. "William likes sitting, crawling, making noise, not napping, and goop on Dad. I'm running out of time to make him a present."

"Smells like he needs a new diaper," Ian said.

William clanked his rattle again.

"Is he trying to make music?" Olivia said. "I wonder . . ."

"Ladies and gentlemen, welcome to a special concert of the Olivia Orchestra with a special guest star, my baby brother William!" Olivia said.
"Ooh! Aah!" the crowd said as William dazzled them with his music. The auditorium filled with applause as William and Olivia took a bow.

"That's it! A xylophone!" Olivia said. "That's the perfect present for William!" She pulled out her trunk to get to work. She just needed a few clinky-sounding things. "And now for the clinky test!" she said, and banged on a few pots. "Hmm, not very clinky."

"Dad, it's almost time for William's party!" Olivia said to her father as he washed dishes in the sink. "And I still need to find something that'll make a—" *Clink-clink!* The spoons clinked against each other in the sink, making the perfect sound. That was it!

"Thanks, Dad!" Olivia said as she ran to make her xylophone.

Olivia put the finishing touches on her xylophone.
"It's almost party time!" Mother called from downstairs.
"Coming!" Olivia said.

Downstairs William's first birthday party was under way. "Okay, William, let's see what Ian got you," Father said.

William cooed as he unwrapped Ian's present—a diaper!

"William can always use a clean diaper!" Ian said.

"That's very thoughtful of you, Ian," Mother said. "Looks like it's time for William's last present. Olivia!" she called.

Olivia handed William her perfectly wrapped present, complete with a bright red bow. "Made especially for you," she said to William.
William unwrapped the homemade xylophone and pushed it aside. He smiled and waved the red-and-white wrapping paper over his head.

"He likes the wrapping paper more than my present," Olivia said, disappointed that her present was a flop. "Well, happy birthday anyway, William." She leaned in to give her baby brother a hug. He reached up and put the bright red bow on her head.

That gave Olivia an idea! "I'll be right back," she said.

A few minutes later Olivia came back downstairs.
"I finally figured out what in the world William wants," she said. "It's me!"

"Wow, what a wonderful gift—the best sister ever!" Mother said.
"Olivia, you did it!" Ian said. "You gave William the perfect present!"
William laughed and squirmed with excitement. "Happy birthday, one-year-old.
I love you!" Olivia said.

"Olivia, you really helped make William's special day extra special," Mother said, tucking her in.

Suddenly, they heard the tinkling of a xylophone from down the hall.

William liked Olivia's first gift after all.

"Operation Perfect Present: complete!" Olivia whispered as she drifted off to sleep.